Dear Reader,

This book was made completely by me, Jake Cake. I did all the words and all the pictures and it took me ages. It's about all the strange things that get me into trouble. Strange things that are SO STRANGE no one EVER believes me.

When I try telling grown-ups what REALLY happened they shake their heads and say: 'DON'T MAKE UP STORIES OR YOUR NOSE WILL GROW LONG!' But I'm not making up stories. Everything I'm about to tell you is true. It all REALLY HAPPENED!

signed Jake Cake

Michael Broad spent much of his childhood gazing out of the window imagining he was somewhere more interesting.

Now he's a grown-up Michael still spends a lot of time gazing out of the window imagining he's somewhere more interesting – but now he writes and illustrates books as well.

Some of them are picture books, like *Broken Bird* and *The Little Star Who Wished*.

Books by Michael Broad

JAKE CAKE: THE FOOTBALL BEAST
JAKE CAKE: THE PIRATE CURSE
JAKE CAKE: THE ROBOT DINNER LADY
JAKE CAKE: THE SCHOOL DRAGON
JAKE CAKE: THE VISITING VAMPIRE
JAKE CAKE: THE WEREWOLF TEACHER

JAKE CAKE

THE FOOTBALL BEAST

Michael Broad

PUFFIN

This book is dedicated
to my friend Craig

PUFFIN BOOKS

Published by the Penguin Group
Penguin Books Ltd, 80 Strand, London WC2R 0RL, England
Penguin Group (USA) Inc., 375 Hudson Street, New York, New York 10014, USA
Penguin Group (Canada), 90 Eglinton Avenue East, Suite 700, Toronto, Ontario, Canada M4P 2Y3
(a division of Pearson Penguin Canada Inc.)
Penguin Ireland, 25 St Stephen's Green, Dublin 2, Ireland (a division of Penguin Books Ltd)
Penguin Group (Australia), 250 Camberwell Road, Camberwell, Victoria 3124, Australia
(a division of Pearson Australia Group Pty Ltd)
Penguin Books India Pvt Ltd, 11 Community Centre, Panchsheel Park, New Delhi – 110 017, India
Penguin Group (NZ), 67 Apollo Drive, Rosedale, North Shore 0632, New Zealand
(a division of Pearson New Zealand Ltd)
Penguin Books (South Africa) (Pty) Ltd, 24 Sturdee Avenue, Rosebank, Johannesburg 2196, South Africa

Penguin Books Ltd, Registered Offices: 80 Strand, London WC2R 0RL, England

puffinbooks.com

First published 2008
1

Set in Perpetua
Made and printed in England by Clays Ltd, St Ives plc

British Library Cataloguing in Publication Data
A CIP catalogue record for this book is available from the British Library

ISBN: 978–0–141–32370–1

www.greenpenguin.co.uk

Mixed Sources
Product group from well-managed
forests and other controlled sources
www.fsc.org Cert no. SA-COC-1592
© 1996 Forest Stewardship Council
FSC

Penguin Books is committed to a sustainable future
for our business, our readers and our planet.
The book in your hands is made from paper
certified by the Forest Stewardship Council.

Here are three UNBELIEVABLE stories about the times I met:

JAKE CAKE
AND THE
Football
BEAST

love watching football on TV and support my local team, who are the best team *ever*, by the way, so when I saw a notice for the new after-school football club I signed up immediately. I was looking forward to the first

evening of practice until I found out
Simon Stokes had already been chosen
as team captain. Simon is really good
at sports so he *always* gets special
treatment.

'Have you come to bake us a cake,
Jake?' Simon yelled, as I ran on to the
pitch. The rest of the boys laughed even
though it wasn't funny, so I reckon they
just wanted to stay on the right side of
the captain.

'That's original,' I mumbled.

A high-pitched whistle shrieked in the distance as Mr Trent sprinted up to us with a net bag full of footballs and a cardboard box. Mr Trent is our school sports teacher but acts like an army sergeant on manoeuvres.

'Right, you lazy bunch of daffodils!' Mr Trent yelled. 'I want a lap of the pitch! GO! GO! GO!'

Simon instantly shot off across the pitch, quickly followed by the rest of the team, and then me. All the other boys were puffing and panting to keep up with the captain, while I was happy to keep a safe distance from any more 'cake' comments.

I was running along the edge of the woods, wondering if after-school football was such a good idea after all, when I saw something large and brown running alongside me through the trees.

I slowed to a jog to get a better look when – *BEEP! BEEP!*

BEEP! BEEP!

The teacher's whistle shrieked behind me and I nearly leapt out of my skin.

'Knees up, Cake!' yelled Mr Trent, sprinting past at high speed.

When I looked back into the woods the creature was gone.

By the time I finished the lap and rejoined the group, Mr Trent was pulling our new team shirts out of the box and calling our names to collect them. The shirt was really cool – red and blue striped – but when I pulled mine on it dropped down to my knees and the sleeves

flapped around my arms
like wings.

It was HUGE!

'Nice dress!'
Simon sniggered,
grinning like a
Cheshire cat.

Simon had
collected everyone's
shirt sizes the week before, and his
sniggering told me he'd deliberately
changed my medium to an XXXL!

Mr Trent rolled his eyes and said I'd
have to make do until a replacement
could be ordered. Then he said it might
not arrive in time for our first match
against City Boys' School at the end of
the week!

HOORAY!

'HOORAY!' everyone cheered, and even I forgot about my shirt.

We were all really excited about our first match and couldn't wait to get some practice in. Mr Trent told Simon to split his team for a five-a-side game, which would have been great, except that there were eleven of us.

No prizes for guessing who didn't get chosen!

While everyone else took to the pitch for five-a-side, I was sent off to the edge to practise my dribbling skills! With the massive shirt flapping around me, I tapped the ball half-heartedly and felt absolutely miserable.

I was thinking that after-school football was *definitely* the worst idea ever when I heard a rustling from the trees. I stopped dribbling the ball and peered into the woods. And there it

was – the large
creature I'd seen
before. It was hiding
behind one of two
small trees and
peeping through
the leaves.

At first I
thought it might be a bear because it
was brown and covered in fur. But it
was completely the wrong shape for a
bear, and I don't think bears
hide behind trees and
peep through leaves.
So I gave a friendly
wave with my flapping
sleeve to let it
know I was friendly.

BEEP! BEEP!

The sound of Mr Trent's whistle ripped through the air again and I froze to the spot. But when I looked back at the pitch I saw he was whistling at one of the players in the five-a-side game, and no one was looking at me at all.

Back in the woods the creature had stepped out from his hiding place and was standing between the two trees — two trees that just happened to be the same

13

width as a pair of goal posts! He bobbed up and down, shuffled from side to side and eagerly watched the football at my feet.

I thought about it for a moment and realized I had two choices. I could dribble the ball along the edge of the pitch on my own and be completely bored, or I could approach the big hairy creature in the woods and risk getting eaten.

BOOT!

I stepped back and booted the football far into the trees and then ran in after it.

It was a pretty good kick, if I say so myself, and as the ball sailed through the air between the two trees I was sure it would be a goal. But suddenly the creature shot sideways, took to the air and caught it! It was a brilliant save – much better than anything I'd seen on the school pitch.

'Nice one!' I said, thinking anyone that good in goal can't be very scary.

'Thanks!' said the creature, standing up with the ball and brushing the dried leaves from his furry legs. That's when I looked down and saw the size of his feet — and knew exactly what kind of creature he was.

'You're a BIGFOOT!' I gasped.

'I am,' said the Bigfoot. 'You're not going to run away, are you?'

'No, I don't think so,' I said. 'My name's Jake.'

'I'm Littlefoot,' said the Bigfoot.

'Littlefoot?' I laughed, thinking he was making a joke.

'No, that really is my name,' said
Littlefoot. 'Because my feet are a bit
small for a Bigfoot.'

'Oh,' I said, thinking other Bigfoot
feet must be massive. 'Do you live in
these woods?'

'No, my family are here for a week on
holiday,' he sighed. 'But we have to stay

hidden all the time, so it's pretty boring. I'm looking forward to going home at the weekend.'

Littlefoot explained that he had found our school pitch and enjoyed watching us play football. He said it reminded him of his friends back home where he was on the local Bigfoot football team.

'I'm supposed to be playing on this team,' I said, nodding back towards the field. 'We've got a big match coming up

matchstick
drawings of
my team
↓

but I'm
not going
to be ready for it
without any proper practice.'

'We can kick a few around,' said
Littlefoot excitedly. 'If you want to?'

He didn't have to ask twice!

While the rest of my team played
five-a-side, I played one-a-side with
the Bigfoot, whose big feet made him
brilliant at dribbling and shooting and
defending the goal, so I had to work

really hard to tackle him and score.

The time whizzed by and before I
knew it Mr Trent blew the whistle to
signal the end of the five-a-side game.

'I'd better go,' I said to a disappointed

Littlefoot, and then ran out of the trees
to rejoin the team.

'Where have you been, Cake?' asked
Mr Trent.

'Er, just retrieving the ball, sir,' I said.
'It rolled into the woods.'

'Then you obviously need more ball
control,' he said.

'He was probably off playing with the

fairies,' Simon sniggered, nudging the other kids to laugh at his joke. 'Or were you making up stories about woodland trolls again?'

'Whatever,' I mumbled, because the woodland trolls were real. I got into loads of trouble last year when they kidnapped the school gerbil and I had to get it back – but I'll tell you about that another time.

The next evening Simon dropped me

from five-a-side again and Mr Trent sent me off to work on my ball control, and this carried on for the rest of the week.

23

I pretended to be disappointed, but was secretly pleased because it meant I could practise with Littlefoot.

After four evenings of one-a-side we were really good friends.

'Same time tomorrow then?' he said, when Mr Trent blew his whistle to mark the end of practice on Thursday.

'It's the big game against City Boys' tomorrow,' I said, making my way back out through

the trees. 'So they'll probably want me to play because it's a proper eleven-a-side match.'

'Well, good luck,' he said. 'I'll be watching and rooting for your team.'

'Thanks,' I said, feeling bad that Littlefoot had to stay hidden and watch the game from the trees. Then I realized I wouldn't get to see him again as he'd be going back home at the weekend.

'Here,' I said, pulling off my massive shirt and running back to hand it to the Bigfoot.

'It'll probably fit you better than me.'
'Won't you get into trouble?' said
Littlefoot, proudly pulling on the shirt.
'I'm always in
trouble anyway,'
I laughed.

I did get into trouble for 'losing' the
massive football shirt, but luckily the
new one arrived in time for the match
on Friday, and it was a perfect fit. Not
that anyone would get to see it, though.

City Boys' were a
man down, so Simon
had to put a player
on the wings.

'Great!' I said,
as I took a seat
on the bench.
Not only was
I not getting
a chance to

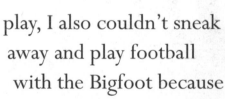

play, I also couldn't sneak
away and play football
with the Bigfoot because
Mr Trent was right
next to me.

'I don't know
why you're
complaining,' Simon

sneered. 'You're the worst player, and
if you want our school to win then
you have to stand back and let the *real*
players do their stuff.'

Our team watched as the City Boys'
team poured off the bus and jogged on
to the pitch, followed by their coach and
what looked from a distance like a giant
shark in a football shirt!

'What's that?' Simon
gasped, as the shark

zigzagged behind the players, clapping and cheering and waving his fins in the air.

'That's their team mascot,' said Mr Trent.

'Why haven't we got a mascot?' the team grumbled to Simon.

Simon went red in the face and shifted uncomfortably because, as team captain, it was his job to keep the players happy.

Then he turned to me and pointed an accusing finger.

'I told Sponge Cake there to sort out the mascot over a week ago!' he yelled.

'Wha—' I gasped, knowing Simon was lying through his teeth.

'Yeah,' he added. 'And all he's done this week is slack off from practice!'

'But —' I said, as the team gathered around looking very disappointed.

'As captain, I say we vote him off the team!' Simon snarled. 'Who's with me?'

I looked up at the team who were about to decide the fate of my future football career, but they weren't listening to Simon any more, they were looking over my head at something in the trees.

'COOL!' they all said at once, while Simon's jaw dropped.

I turned to see Littlefoot zigzagging out of the trees, clapping and cheering and waving his hairy arms in the air. He was wearing the massive team shirt I'd given him and looked like the best team mascot EVER!

'Did you do this, Jake?' asked Mr
Trent, stepping up to the Bigfoot,
straightening his shirt and looking really
impressed for the first time ever.

'Er, yes, sir,' I said, smiling at
Littlefoot. 'My mum sewed the costume.'

'Well, you've done a marvellous job!'
he said, and the whole team cheered.

Simon *could* have taken some credit
for having chosen me to sort out the
mascot, even though he hadn't. But
he was so annoyed that I was getting
cheered that he pushed past the team
and marched up to Littlefoot.

'What's it supposed to *be*, anyway?' he
snapped.

'Um, it's a Bigfoot,' I said. 'A football
Bigfoot.'

'That's stupid,' Simon sneered,

standing on
tiptoes to
peer into
Littlefoot's
eyes. 'Who's
in there,
anyway?
Your mum?'

Simon laughed and looked back at
the team, expecting them to laugh with
him. But no one did because everyone
thought the new mascot was cool. Even
Mr Trent seemed disappointed with
Simon for being so mean-spirited.

'My friend Li-Liam offered to help
out,' I stammered.

'Well, I think it's the dumbest thing
I've ever seen and I refuse to play with

that thing running up and down the
pitch!' said Simon, stepping up to the
team. 'Who's with
me?'

The team all folded their arms and
looked awkwardly at Mr Trent.

'I'm with you,' said Mr Trent. 'I agree
that you shouldn't play . . .'

Simon gave me his meanest sneer
while Littlefoot and the team sighed
heavily.

'. . . and I think Jake should take your

place,' finished Mr Trent.

'Wha—' gasped Simon.

'Anyone who has been kept out of the five-a-side games all week and still goes to so much effort for the team *deserves* to play,' said Mr Trent. 'And I think you need to sit on the bench and think about what makes a good sportsman.'

'But I'm the team captain!' yelled Simon.

'Not any more,' said Mr Trent. He plucked the captain's badge off Simon's shirt

PLUCK!

The captain badge ↙

and pinned it firmly on mine. 'Now, let's see how we get on with a captain with real team spirit.'

I'd like to say that the team cheered when I was chosen as captain. That's what would have happened in a movie,

but everyone still looked awkward. Simon had spent the whole week telling everyone I was rubbish at football, and as I'd missed practice and only really played with a Bigfoot, I wasn't sure either.

Simon
Scowling

Simon sat scowling at me throughout the whole match, but not because he'd been kept on the wings. He scowled because, to everyone's surprise, I was actually *really* good!

Having spent the whole week tackling a huge player with massive feet, regular-

sized players with regular-sized feet
were a doddle! I weaved in and out
and ran rings around the City Boys',
while Littlefoot cheered me on (and
occasionally chased the shark around
the pitch).

By the final whistle I'd scored three
goals and made passes to my team
that scored another five, including the
winning goal!

We thrashed City Boys', and the team
lifted Littlefoot and me on to their
shoulders for a winning parade. Simon
was completely fuming and kicked the
bench in protest. But he must have
kicked it too hard because when he
came to school the following week he
had a BIG FOOT of his own!

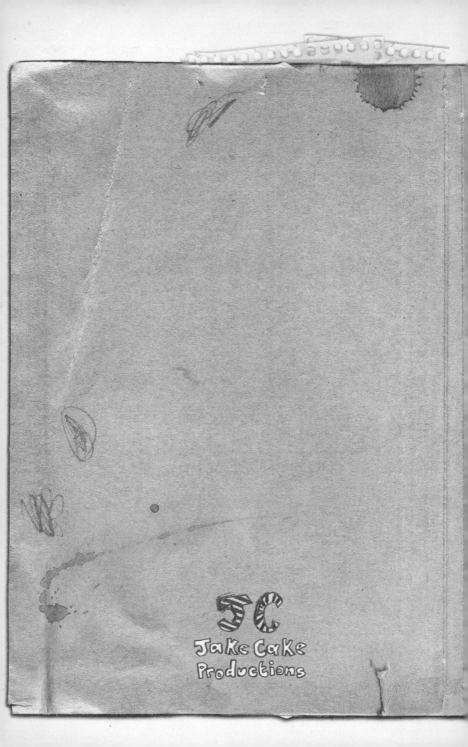

JC

Jake Cake
Productions

JAKE CAKE
AND THE
SEA
MonsteR

6'6"	6'6"
6'0"	6'0"
5'6"	5'6"
5'0"	5'0"
4'6"	4'6"
4'0"	4'0"
3'6"	3'6"
3'0"	3'0"

'What am I meant to do with these?' I said, frowning at the plastic bucket and spade.

'Build a sandcastle, of course,' Mum said, setting up the windbreak and laying out her beach towel. 'All the

other kids have
them and
they're not
complaining.'
  I looked at
the other kids building
sandcastles and they were
all half my age. I think
Mum was trying to
teach me a lesson
or something
because I'd spent
half the drive to the seaside
begging for an inflatable surfboard.
And when Mum said they were too
dangerous because I might get swept
away, I spent the other half sulking.

'I'm too old for sandcastles,' I said flatly.

'And yet still young enough to sulk when you don't get your own way,' Mum sighed, plonking herself down on the towel. 'You don't *have* to build sandcastles. There are plenty of other things to do.'

'Can I bury you in the sand?' I asked, eagerly waving the plastic spade.

'Absolutely not!' Mum said. 'I want to get a nice tan for the summer.'

'Then I'll dig for crabs instead,' I suggested.

'CRABS!' Mum gasped. 'You *know* how I feel about crabs!'

Mum is terrified of crabs because one nipped her toe when

she was little. She even squeals when they're shown on TV and hides behind a cushion until they've gone.

'Then can I have a s–' I was about to make one more plea for the inflatable surfboard, but Mum must be a mind reader because she quickly interrupted me.

'If you say *surfboard* one more time, we're going home!' she snapped.

Um...

'Um, I was only going to ask for a sandwich,' I lied.

'Not until lunchtime,' Mum said firmly.

'If I open the box now they'll get covered in sand and we don't want sandwiches with sand in them.'

'All *sand*wiches have *sand* in them,' I joked. 'That's how they're spelled.'

Mum dipped her sunglasses and glared at me over the top, which meant she wasn't in a joking mood. I did hear someone else chuckling, though, but when I looked around I couldn't see who it was.

That's odd! I thought.

Mum didn't notice because she was too busy rummaging inside the beach bag.

'Why don't you play with this?' she said, pulling out my snorkel and dangling it in front of me. 'The last time we had a day at the seaside you spent half the journey begging for it and the other half sulking until you got your own way.'

The determined
look on Mum's
face told me I
would not get
my own way
this time, so
I reluctantly
took the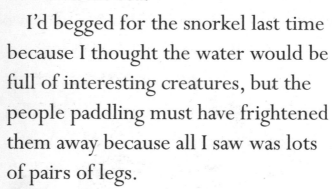
snorkel and wandered
down to the sea.

I'd begged for the snorkel last time
because I thought the water would be
full of interesting creatures, but the
people paddling must have frightened
them away because all I saw was lots
of pairs of legs.

This time there were lots of pairs
of legs again, so I swam further out,

hoping to find an ancient shipwreck or
an underwater city. I did see something
that looked like a sea witch, but it was
just a rock with seaweed
sprouting from
the top.

I know what a sea witch looks like because I met one once at the local aquarium. I got into loads of trouble when she flooded the gift shop – but I'll tell you about that another time.

I splashed around in the sea for a while and then made my way back up the beach, hoping it was close enough to lunchtime for Mum to crack open the sandwiches. But as I got closer to our stripy windbreak I found Mum

replaced by a large mound
of sand!

On closer inspection I
found Mum *beneath* the sand
mound with her face neatly framed at
the top. She was snoring her head off.

'Mum?' I said, a bit annoyed that she
hadn't let me bury her because she'd
obviously wanted to do it herself. Mum
didn't answer because the
sand was covering her
ears so I picked up
the plastic spade and
gave the mound
a little prod.

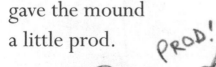

PROD!

The snoring stopped with an abrupt
snuffle and Mum's eyebrows frowned
above her sunglasses. Then she slowly
lifted her head, saw the mound of
sand and leapt up, causing a sandy
avalanche!

'How *could* you?' she
screamed, eyeing the
spade in my hand.

'But, I didn't . . .'
I pleaded.

Mum shook her
head angrily and
then stomped
down to the
water to wash
off the thick layer of sand that was stuck
to her suntan lotion. I looked at the

spade and realized
Mum had every
reason to think I'd
buried her.

'Chuckle!
Chuckle!'
chuckled a
nearby voice.

'Who is that?'
I asked, looking
around to find no
one there again.

Mum returned dripping wet, shook
the sand from her buried beach towel
and patted herself dry. I said nothing
because there was nothing I could say
that would convince Mum I hadn't
buried her.

'What a waste of suntan lotion!'
Mum grumbled, sitting down and
reaching for the beach bag. 'Honestly,
Jake, I sometimes wonder if you do
these things on purpose just to –'

Mum didn't get to finish the sentence

because at that moment the bag tipped
over and a dozen tiny crabs
tumbled into her lap! The
next thing she said was
'ARRRRRGH!' and legged
it halfway down the beach.
   'Chuckle! Chuckle!'
chuckled the voice again.

the crabs
were cute

By now I was certain the invisible chuckler was responsible for the burial *and* the crabs, so I walked around the towel and peered behind the windbreak. But after searching all over he was nowhere to be found.

I collected the crabs in the plastic bucket and released them into the sea. Then I had to go and fetch Mum. It took me a while but I eventually convinced her that the crabs were all gone and led her back along the beach.

Instead of the tan she was
hoping for, Mum looked very pale so I
suggested an early lunch. Mum agreed,
but I could tell she was still cross with
me. There was nothing I could say
because I'd mentioned the sand burial
and the crabs earlier, and they'd both
mysteriously happened.

I was wondering what else I'd
mentioned, when
Mum produced
two plastic plates
and dished out the
sandwiches.

'*Sand*wiches!'
I gasped.

It was too
late. Mum had
taken a bite
from the first
sandwich and
her face froze
mid-munch. I heard the crunch from
where I was sitting and watched with
horror as the sand poured from the half-
bitten bread.

I lifted the corner
of the sandwich on
my plate and found
it was not just a
little sandy – the

62

filling had been carefully removed and
replaced with a handful of the stuff!

'I think I'll pop to that little shop
and buy us some more sandwiches,'
Mum said calmly and quietly, which is
always more scary than her yelling. She
dropped the remains of the sandwich
on to the plate and wiped her mouth
with a napkin. 'And when we've
eaten those, we're
going home.'

Mum took her purse and left me on
the towel to think about what I'd done,
even though I hadn't done it. And if *I*
hadn't done it . . .

'Chuckle! Chuckle!'

This time when the chuckler
chuckled, I was looking at a mound of
sand and I saw it tremble slightly. Then

the mound shifted
as the underground
thing hurried away.
It reminded me
of my cat Fatty
when he tunnels
under my duvet.

I quickly
grabbed the
plastic spade
and followed it,
determined to
find out what had
got me into trouble. When the fleeing
mound paused under Mum's towel I
whacked it with the spade.

'Come out where I can see you!' I
demanded.

The thing below the sand was still for
a moment before it spoke.

'I'm too scary,' it said. 'You'll run
away screaming. Everyone does.'

'I'm not everyone,' I said, because
I've seen lots of scary things in my
unbelievable adventures and you kind of
get used to it. And, besides, I was much
too angry to be scared. 'Show yourself
now or you'll get another whack!'

The thing sighed and shifted, then a
massive head peeped out from under

the towel. It was obviously a monster because it was green and lumpy and had big yellow teeth, and it *was* pretty scary-looking. But to be honest, I've seen worse.

I realized the other people on the beach probably *hadn't* seen worse and, not wanting to add a stampede to my list of beach crimes, I quickly moved the windbreak to hide it from view.

'You're a sand monster!' I said, waving the spade in case he made any sudden moves. 'No, I'm actually a sea monster,' he said. 'I moved to the sand because the sea is really boring. I tried playing with the legs, but they kept running back up to the beach.'

'So now you hide under the sand and play tricks on people?' I said.

'I have to stay hidden or people will run away again,' he explained. 'But I only want someone to play with.

It's lonely
being the only
monster and
very difficult
to make friends.'

'Then why did you
get me into trouble?' I asked, thinking it
was a really bad way to make friends. 'I
heard you chuckling.'

'Your *sand*wich joke made me laugh,'
said the monster. 'So I tried to make
you laugh too by doing the things that
you said. I didn't
mean to get you
into trouble.
I thought it
would be
funny.'

I suppose it would have been funny
if I hadn't been blamed, so I put the
spade down. The sea monster was
obviously friendly and I felt sorry for
him being lonely and having to hide in
the sand.

'I would play with you,' I said, 'but
I'm pretty sure my mum's taking me
home soon. And we probably won't be
back for a while, especially after the

burial and the crabs and the sand sandwiches.'

The sea monster nodded sadly.

Mum was heading back with our lunch so I told the monster to hide again.

'I'll try to get my mum to stay longer, but I can't promise anything because she's very cross with me,' I whispered. 'If I can talk her round, I'll meet you in the sea after lunch.'

The head-shaped mound nodded and then slowly shrank beneath the sand.

'And no more *crabs*!' I hissed after him.

As Mum returned with the non-sand sandwiches I prepared myself for some serious begging. But not for an inflatable surfboard – this time I'd be begging forgiveness for things I hadn't done.

I have to say the begging was very hard work and I had to use various different strategies. I began with apologies and promises of future good behaviour. Then I moved on to guilt and regret

for everything
I'd done. And to
clinch the deal
I ended with
flattery.

'. . . I'd feel
really bad if we
went home
before you got
a nice suntan,'

I sighed, 'because it
always makes you
look so pretty.'

'Really?' Mum
smiled. 'A suntan
makes me look
pretty?'

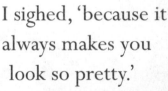

'And young,' I added, which was my final ace card.

I waited eagerly for the verdict.

'Well, I have to say I'm *very* impressed,' Mum said, reaching for the suntan lotion. 'I think it's very grown up of you to take responsibility for your actions, and to think of others for a change.'

'Does that mean we can stay?' I asked.

'Yes,' said Mum, already rubbing the smelly sun protection into her arms.

I ran down the beach
and waded into the water
as quickly as I could. The
apology negotiations had
gone on longer
than I expected
and I was worried
the sea monster
had given up
waiting.

I swam
through the
sea of legs and out into the deeper
water, then I scanned the depths for
something that looked like a monster.
I'd only seen the sea monster's head,
so I wasn't sure how big he was or what
the rest of him looked like.

Then I saw a dark blue shape sitting
on the seabed and peering up at me.

I waved and coaxed him to the
surface, and was very impressed when
he unravelled his tentacles and soared
through the water towards me. I would
have been terrified if I hadn't
known he was friendly.

'Hello!' I said, as his head
bobbed just above the
water. 'I made it!'

'Are you talking
to me?' The sea
monster
frowned
and
glanced
behind him.

'Of course,' I laughed. 'There's no one else around.'

'And you're not going to swim away screaming?' he asked.

'No,' I said. 'Didn't we cover this earlier?'

The sea monster frowned and scratched his head with a tentacle.

'In the sand!' I said. 'With the burial and the crabs and the *sand*wiches?'

The monster slowly shook his mighty head.

'You *are* the sea monster who moved to the sand to make friends?' I asked cautiously.

'No,' said the monster awkwardly. 'I'm the *sand* monster who moved to the *sea* to make friends.'

It was then that I noticed something odd. Instead of two little fins sticking out of its head, there were two little spades, meaning this was a completely different monster altogether.

GULP!

Suddenly a second giant head popped out of the water, and this one *did* have

two little fins. Although, aside from that difference, the monsters looked exactly the same.

'Sorry I'm late,' said the sea monster, and then stared wide-eyed when he saw the sand monster bobbing beside me. And the sand monster looked just as startled by the sea monster!

It was obvious to me that these two monsters had never met before, and as I'd met both of them it was left to me to make the formal introductions.

'Sea monster, this is sand monster,'
I said, nodding from fin-head to spade-
head. 'Sand monster, this is sea monster,'
I added, nodding from spade-head to
fin-head.

Both monsters shyly extended a
tentacle and shook them politely, and
it was then that I spotted something I
hadn't noticed before. My *old* friend

sea monster was blushing really badly and my *new* friend sand monster was batting her eyelashes.

Spade-head was a lady monster!

Both lonely monsters were obviously very pleased to meet each other and spent quite a long time exchanging stories. They also quickly worked out that they'd swapped homes during the same summer and must have just missed each other.

I was very happy for them, but I was also getting bored.

'Er, I don't want to interrupt,' I said, waving at the pair of chatting monsters, 'but my legs are getting a bit tired from treading water, so I think I should go back to the beach –'

'Don't go!' they both said together. 'We haven't had a chance to play yet.'

With this the two monsters ducked under the water and the next thing I knew I was rising out of the sea like Neptune! I looked down and saw my feet planted firmly on the monsters' heads.

'WOW!' I gasped, and then realized
everyone could see me standing on
water.

I quickly looked back at the beach.
Mum was stretched out in the sun, and
none of the paddlers were looking at me
because there were loads of other kids
standing on surfboards.

'Hold on tight!' the monsters said
together.

With this they shot through the water

at high speed,
and even though
I didn't have
anything to
hold on to,
I still
managed
to keep
my balance
most of the time.

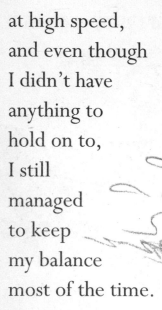

The times I did fall off,
a handy tentacle scooped me out of the
water and set me upright again.

Forget inflatable surfboards – monster
surfing is the best water sport EVER!

Luckily I was treading water when
Mum called me in from the beach, but
before I swam back to shore the sea

monster told me to wait and shot away
towards the deep
dark ocean.
    He returned
moments
later with a
small brown
rock.
    'This is for your mum,' said
the sea monster, looking very pleased
with himself, 'to say
sorry for everything.
And it will make her
happy and not cross
with you any more.'
    'Are you sure?'
I asked, frowning
at the rock.

85

The sea monster nodded and I promised to give it to her.

Back on the beach Mum was packing the bag, and it was taking her quite a long time because she was checking everything for crabs.

'I got you this from the sea to say sorry,' I said, because saying it came

from a sea monster would have just
got me into more trouble and a lecture
about making up stories.

'Oh, a rock!' Mum said, trying to
look pleased. Then she held it up to
eye level, tipped her sunglasses and
frowned. 'Actually, it's not a rock at all.
It's a crusty old clam!'

Great! I thought.
Even worse than a rock!

'I wonder . . .' Mum said, tapping the brown lump with her knuckle and trying to prise it open with her fingers. None of these things worked so she put it down and whacked it with my spade.

The two halves of the shell cracked open.

'Oh, Angel Cake!' Mum squealed, plucking out the shiny white pearl.

Mum grabbed me and gave

PEARL!

me a massive
embarrassing
hug, but I
didn't mind
because I
was glad she was
happy again. And
looking over her
shoulder I could
just make out two
tentacles waving on the horizon.

JC
Jake Cake
Productions

JAKE CAKE

AND THE

Funfair

Phantom

'But it looks rubbish!' I said, frowning at the rundown ghost train and comparing it to the cooler rides at the funfair. The cool rides were huge and fast and everyone was

screaming. The ghost train was deserted
like a ghost *town*! 'Can't I have another
go on the Dinosaur Dipper or the
Rocket Launcher?' I pleaded.

'We queued
for hours to
get on those
rides,'
Mum
said,
tearing

off a ride-token and handing it to the
woman in the ghost-train booth. 'And
this one has no queues at all!'

'I wonder why,' I said, reluctantly
taking a seat on the empty train.

Mum never goes on rides because
they make her feel sick, so she waved
enthusiastically as the train crawled
towards two rusty doors. The doors had
Tunnel of Terror written above them in
blood-red lettering.

'I'll be the judge of that!' I mumbled, folding my arms defiantly. I've been on loads of ghost trains before and they're never, *ever* scary.

The doors slammed behind me and the train rattled along the track, taking a sharp right turn where a green plastic skeleton bounced up and down on a piece of elastic.

'YAWN!' I yawned.

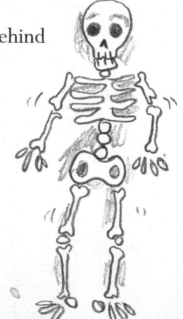

The train carried
on through the
darkness and at
the next turn
there was a
coffin with a
creaky lid. As
the lid creaked
open a plastic vampire rose slightly and
then flopped back down again with a
hollow clunk.

'YAWN!' I yawned
again.

The third turn
revealed a flapping
white
sheet
that was

97

probably supposed to be a ghost, but
it was about as scary as a white sheet
hanging on a windy washing line.

'BORING!' I sighed,
batting a rubber bat
that dangled over
my head.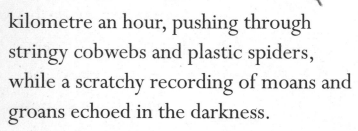

The train
continued to
chug along
at about one
kilometre an hour, pushing through
stringy cobwebs and plastic spiders,
while a scratchy recording of moans and
groans echoed in the darkness.

'They're probably moaning and
groaning out of boredom!' I chuckled.

My chuckle was cut short when the

train suddenly stopped with a jolt that made me jump. Then a bright blue phantom appeared on the track in front of me! 'I'm doing my best,' he growled. 'You don't have to make fun of it!'

I wasn't sure whether to scream or say sorry because he wasn't very scary and looked pretty upset. But the phantom vanished before I had a chance to do either and the next thing I knew the train had started up again.

99

Judging by the poor quality of frights in the *Tunnel of Terror* I was certain the phantom was real. And I knew he was a phantom because he was a bit see-through like a ghost. Phantoms are very similar to ghosts – except they're monster-shaped instead of people-shaped.

It also made sense that a phantom would live in a ghost-train ride because all they're good for is scaring people. Although this one wasn't even good at that judging by the lack of queues!

By the time I'd worked all this out the train had passed a shop

↑
dummy
mummy

CACKLE!
CACKLE!

dummy with bits of
bandage draped over
it that was supposed
to be a mummy, a
cackling witch with
flashing light bulbs for
eyes and a balding
werewolf with
a missing fang.

one
FANG

The train
was now chugging
towards the exit and
as it crashed through the
doors into daylight I was
pretty confused. How could a phantom
living in a ghost train be so bad at
scaring people?

'You look like you've seen a

101

spooooooky ghost!'
Mum gasped
dramatically, as
the train ground
to a halt.

'I saw a sheet,' I said sarcastically.

I decided not to tell Mum about the
phantom because she'd just assume it
was part of the ride, and if I insisted he
was real she'd think I couldn't tell the
difference between a monster and a
dummy.

'I've just made an appointment to

see the
fortune-teller!'
Mum said
excitedly,
pointing
to a nearby
tent with stars and
moons all over it. 'But
we need to hurry — the planets will be
aligned for my reading in five minutes'
time.'

'That's convenient,' I mumbled,
because I don't believe fortune-tellers
can *really* tell the future. I think they just
say nice things so that people go away
feeling happy.

The last time Mum went to see the
funfair fortune-teller it went on for

ages, but that
was mostly
because I
kept laughing
and doing
impressions
of Madam Mystic.

Madam Mystic said Mum would
have a lot of trouble with a certain boy
who couldn't take things seriously.

I wonder who she was talking about?

'Can't I stay on the ghost train?' I
asked. It had to be better than Madam
Mystic, and I was still very curious
about the funfair phantom. 'It's actually
quite good and we do have four ride-
tokens left.'

At the mention of four tokens the

woman in the ghost-train booth hurried
over.

'I can keep an eye on him for you,'
she said enthusiastically.

'Oh, I couldn't ask you to do that,'
Mum said, frowning at her watch.

'It would be my pleasure,' said the

 woman. 'The
funfair are
closing us
down after
today, so it
would be
nice to see
the old girl
rattle round
a few more times before she goes into
retirement.'

'Closing
down?' Mum
said. 'But why?'
'We can't
compete with
the bigger rides,'
the woman said sadly.
'It would seem ghost trains
are rather old-fashioned and not exciting
enough for young people today.'
'I'm terribly sorry,' Mum said.
'So can I stay here?' I
pleaded.
'Oh, all right,'
Mum sighed,
handing the
tickets to the
woman.

'Now, if he gives you any trouble at all, or starts making up stories about monsters, I'll be just inside that tent.'

Before leaving, Mum warned me to behave myself for the nice lady and not to make fun of the ghost train any more. Then she hurried off to the fortune-teller's tent to have her future told.

The woman started up the ride again and waved at me as the train chugged towards the doors. I felt bad for making fun of the ghost train, especially now I knew it was closing down. But as the doors slammed and the green skeleton bounced

around in front of me again I could
definitely see why.

It just *wasn't* scary!

As the carriage crawled past the
coffin and the sheet I looked out for the
phantom, but when the train stopped this
time, he didn't appear. It was then that I
heard a strange noise over the recording
of moaning and groaning.

It sounded like sobbing.

 The train
carried on,
moving
away
from the
sound,
so I leapt
out of the

carriage and walked
back up the track.
The tunnels
were lined with
sheets of black
cloth and
when I pulled
one back I
found the
blue phantom in a
secret room.

The room obviously wasn't part of
the ride. In fact it looked like a pretty
nice kid's bedroom, with a bed and a
desk and shelves of books; it even had
a small TV in the corner. The phantom
was sitting on the bed and when he saw
me he sniffed and wiped his eyes.

'Have you come to make fun of
the scares again?' he asked.

'Er, no,' I said, realizing for the first
time that the phantom was about my
age, which I think is
pretty young in
phantom years
because some
of them have
been around
for centuries.

'Actually, I wanted to say sorry.'

'It's OK,' he sniffed, blowing his nose loudly on a tissue. 'You were right anyway. The scares *are* boring, and now they're closing the ride down because I can't make anyone scream. And kids only go on the rides with the loudest screams.'

'I could scream,' I suggested. 'If you think it would help.'

'One scream can't compete with the Dinosaur Dipper or the Rocket Launcher,' said the phantom. 'But thanks for offering, and for not laughing at me when I jumped in front of the train.'

'Why would I laugh?'
I asked.

'That's what
kids used to
do before
the big rides
came,' he said. 'I tried to be scary, but
they thought I was just someone in a
silly blue suit. Some even threw their
candyfloss and toffee apples at me,
which wasn't very nice.'
Suddenly the black
curtain flapped back.
'What on earth!'
gasped the woman
from the ghost-train
booth, moving her
head between the

phantom and me and looking pretty
terrified.

'It's OK,' I said, realizing the sight of
a phantom might be a bit much for a
grown-up. 'He's very friendly –'

'I know *he's* friendly!' snapped the
woman. 'But what about you? As soon
as the empty train came out I *knew* you'd
be snooping around and causing trouble.
Your mother
warned me.'

'Uh?' I said, because I couldn't work out what was going on.

'Oh dear!' she gasped. 'Now everyone will find out about my Bluey.'

'It's OK, Mum,' said the phantom, hurrying over to comfort the woman.

I couldn't work out how a woman could have a phantom for a kid, but they both looked scared, which was probably a first for *this* ghost train. And the thing they were scared of was me telling Mum about the phantom.

'I won't tell,' I smiled. 'Mum wouldn't believe me anyway – she never does.'

'What do you mean?' said the woman, slowly calming down.

'Oh, I see weird stuff all the time,' I said casually.

Bluey's mum explained that she'd inherited the young phantom along with the ghost train, and decided to adopt him as she didn't have any children of her own. Then I told them all about my unbelievable adventures to reassure them I was OK.

'In fact this was probably the *least*

scary thing that's happened to me!'
I said.

'Thanks a lot,' sighed Bluey.

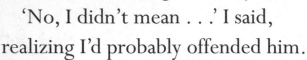

'No, I didn't mean . . .' I said,
realizing I'd probably offended him.

'It's OK.' Bluey's mum smiled and
ruffled the phantom's hair. 'I guess some
phantoms are just naturally scary, while
others are not. And I wouldn't want
you any other way.'

'Actually,' I said, 'I think phantoms can be whatever they want to be.'

'What?' they both said together.

I told them about the time I met a shape-shifting phantom in the local pet shop. He turned from a goldfish into a tiger to scare me away – but I'll tell *you* about that another time.

'I can't shape-shift,' said the phantom.

'Have you ever tried?' I asked.

'Of course not,' he said. 'I wouldn't know how.'

PHANTOM

GOLDFISH

'Well, the one in the pet shop seemed to concentrate when he did it,' I said, remembering how strange it was to see a concentrating goldfish. 'You could always give it a go.'

'What should I concentrate on?' he asked.

'I've got an idea!' I said, and quickly led Bluey and his mum to the section of the ghost train with the balding werewolf. 'Now concentrate on him – but you might want to imagine you have two fangs instead of one.'

The phantom furrowed his brow in concentration.
At first nothing happened, then his body suddenly shifted shape and two wolf ears popped out of his head. This was quickly followed by a long wolf

snout and two white fangs.

Bluey was still small, but now he was
brown and wolfy, and he looked pretty
pleased with himself. His mum was
pleased too because she was jumping up
and down and clapping her hands.

'Now if you want to look like a real
werewolf, you need to be bigger,' I said.

Bluey immediately grew taller, his shoulders bulked out and his teeth doubled in size. Then he lifted his head back and howled at the top of his voice, which made the train tracks vibrate.

The phantom's mum and I took a big step back,

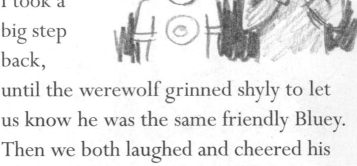

until the werewolf grinned shyly to let us know he was the same friendly Bluey. Then we both laughed and cheered his success.

The phantom made his way around the track, shape-shifting into *scary* versions of the witch and the ghost and the vampire and the skeleton, while his mum carried the old ones away. And when I explained to Bluey that monsters can look like anything, things got really scary as he started making his own frightening creations.

There was one with dragon wings and massive claws! There was another with three heads and the body of a snake!

And the scariest of all was a huge
spider-bat that leapt from the ceiling!

'There's only one thing left
to do,' said the phantom's
mum, dusting her hands
in a businesslike fashion.
'And that's to give the
new *Tunnel of Terror*
a test run! Are you
ready, Bluey?'

The phantom
had changed back to normal and looked
nervous. The tunnels were now empty
apart from a few cobwebs and plastic
spiders, so it was up to him to provide
all the frights.

He took a deep breath and nodded
bravely.

I was pretty nervous too as we took
a seat in the train outside, but I was
sure Bluey could do it. As the train
rattled towards the rusty old doors,
the phantom's mum and I exchanged

anxious looks and then gripped
the safety bar.

When the doors slammed behind
us Bluey went to work.

The huge horned skeleton clattered
over the top of the train, quickly
followed by the three-headed snake.

The vampire swooped from the
shadows and as his cape flapped he
turned into
the roaring
dragon,
shooting
flames
from his
nostrils!

'ARRRRRRRGH!' we screamed.

There was a moment of blackness when we saw a headless ghost running towards us, but then it turned into the

witch and shrieked over our heads. As we looked back the spider-bat suddenly flew towards us, causing us to duck down in our seats!

'ARRRRRRRGH!' we screamed again.

As the train rattled towards the last

stretch we both looked round to see the mummy grinning in the seat between us, then he leapt on to the track and landed as the huge werewolf, snarling and drooling and howling at the top of its voice.

'ARRRRRRRGH!' we screamed, and this scream lasted until the doors slammed behind us and we were back in the daylight.

'That was the best ride EVER!' I said to Bluey's mum.

127

At first I thought Bluey's mum had gone into shock because she was staring at me with wide eyes and her mouth was hanging open. Then I saw that she was looking past me at the people queuing at the ticket booth.

There was a line of parents and  kids trailing back as far as I could see, all itching to go on the ride we'd just taken. The roaring dragon and shrieking witch and howling werewolf, combined with our deafening screams, had brought people from all the way across the funfair!

Looking back at the exit doors we saw a tiny blue thumbs-up

through the gap. We gave Bluey an excited thumbs-up back, and then his mum hurried off to the ticket booth.

I was about to climb out of the train when I saw *my* mum charge from the fortune-teller's tent. She glanced around in a panic at the commotion outside, then she saw me sitting on the train amid the chaos and rolled her eyes.

'What have you been up to now?'
Mum demanded, and marched over
to the ticket-booth. She was about to
offer the usual apologies for my bad
behaviour, but the phantom's mum
spoke first.

'There you are!' she said cheerfully.
'However can I thank you?'

'*Thank* me?' Mum said, as I climbed

down from the train and joined them.

'Yes,' she said, patting my shoulder.
'Your son told me how to make my
ghost train scary again, and now people
are *queuing* to take a ride. There's no
way they'll make us close down now!'

'Really?' Mum said, obviously in
shock.

'What a wonderful imagination he
has,' the phantom's mum added, and
gave me a wink.

'Yes,' Mum said. 'I
suppose he has.'

'I'm sorry, I really must serve these customers,' Bluey's mum apologized, hurrying back behind the booth. 'But please come back soon – you'll have as many free passes as you can use.'

'Thank you,' Mum said, and led me away as the ride started up again.

Bluey must have been enjoying himself because we could hear the roaring and howling and satisfied shrieks all the way out

132

to the car park. It was only then that Mum found her voice again.

'Oh, I forgot to mention,' Mum gasped excitedly. 'Madam Mystic said the crystal ball clearly showed a lady with a young son having a dramatic change in fortune!'

'Really?' I said. 'I wonder who she meant?'

'Well, *I* think it must have been me and you!' Mum added. 'Madam Mystic couldn't say for sure, of course. But she did say the colour blue would be very lucky indeed.'

And I smiled to myself as the ghost train screamed in the distance.

Jake Cake
Productions

UNBELIEVABLE ADVENTURE REPORT

OFFICIAL JC DOCUMENT

NAME: Littlefoot (the BIGFoot)

AGE: about the same age as me

WEIGHT: TONS! (but bigger!)

How To Spot One. Look for something big and brown in the woods (but make sure it's not a Bear!)

Comments:
Littlefoot was very nice and brilliant at football. I hope he comes back next year for his family holiday so we can kick a few around again!

JC
Jake Cake
Productions

UNBELIEVABLE ADVENTURE REPORT

OFFICIAL JC DOCUMENT

NAME: Sea Monster

AGE: Er... don't know.

WEIGHT: Quite a lot - he was HUGE!

How To Spot One look in the sea (or the sand)

Comments: I'm glad that the sea monster made friends with the sand monster. I will look out for them next time I go to the seaside because MONSTER SURFING is the coolest water sport!!!

UNBELIEVABLE ADVENTURE REPORT

NAME: Bluey (the phantom)

AGE: about my age I think

WEIGHT: about my weight I think

How To Spot One. Look in a ghost train - or in a goldfish bowl!

Comments: Most phantoms are not very nice because they like scaring people. But Bluey was scaring people who wanted to be scared so he was very nice. His mum was nice too.

JC
Jake Cake
Productions

Read all the unbelievable adventures of

JAKE CAKE

that's me ↑

I did all the writing and all the drawing